STORIES FROM EAST HIGH #11

KT-408-917

IN THE SPOTLIGHT

By Catherine Hapka

Based on the Disney Channel Original Movie
"High School Musical," Written by Peter Barsocchini
Based on "High School Musical 2,"
Written by Peter Barsocchini
Based on Characters Created by Peter Barsocchini

PaRragon

Bath・New York・Singapore・Hong Kong・Cologne・Delhi・Melbourne

This edition published by Parragon in 2009
Parragon
Queen Street House
4 Queen Street
Bath BA1 1HE, UK

ISBN 978-1-4075-6002-1

Printed in UK

CHAPTER ONE

"**G**o wide, Bolton!" Chad Danforth exclaimed, dribbling his basketball down the school hallway.

Troy Bolton grinned at his best friend. It was Friday morning, before homeroom, and the halls of East High were crowded with students. "I'm open!" he called. Troy dodged a passing sophomore and lifted both hands over his head.

Chad whizzed the ball toward him. Just then, Jason Cross leaped for the interception, but Troy

1

caught the ball easily. He dribbled around Jason and threw it to Zeke Baylor. The foursome were not only friends – they were also teammates on the Wildcats basketball team.

"Can't you give it a rest already?" someone shouted. "You guys can play basketball while we're off from school next week. Do you have to turn the hallway into an obstacle course, too?"

Troy turned and saw that Taylor McKessie, Martha Cox, Kelsi Nielsen and Gabriella Montez had just appeared around the corner. Taylor, who had just yelled at them, had her arms crossed over her chest and her lips pursed as she glared at the guys – especially Chad. Taylor was an excellent student and took school *very* seriously. She didn't have much patience for people who didn't feel the same way, although she'd loosened up a little bit since getting to know Chad better. Still, sometimes she thought he could be very immature.

While Chad tried to defend their ball playing, Troy and Gabriella looked at one another and smiled. Troy thought Gabriella was the most amazing girl he'd ever met. Luckily for him, she thought he was just as special. The two of them had become good friends ever since they'd co-starred in the school's winter musical the previous year.

"Hey," Troy said, stepping toward her.

"Hey, yourself," Gabriella replied, her brown eyes sparkling. "And Taylor's right. Thanks to those teacher conferences and emergency school repairs to the roof, you'll have four whole days next week to play basketball from morning to night."

"Too bad they didn't just give us the whole week off," Chad complained. He dribbled the ball in a circle around himself. "I mean, what's the point of making us come in on Monday when we're off for the rest of the week? What if we wanted to take the time to go somewhere on vacation or something?"

"Yeah, right." Jason snorted and reached out to steal the ball. "Were you planning to use your allowance to jet off to Tibet for some mountain climbing?"

"Nah. Tibet's not really my style." Chad grinned and snatched the ball back. "I was thinking more like windsurfing in Jamaica." He spun the ball around and shot it at the girls. "Think fast, Gabriella!"

"Oh!" Gabriella hadn't been expecting the pass. She grabbed for the ball, but it bounced off her fingertips and bonked Kelsi in the shoulder. "Oops! I'm so sorry, Kelsi!" Gabriella cried, her cheeks turning pink.

"Uh-oh! Butterfingers!" Chad exclaimed with a laugh.

"Good thing there weren't any NBA scouts around, Gabriella," Zeke teased.

"Yeah. You'd never get a contract with the Lakers if they saw that fumble," Jason added, giving her a kind smile.

Gabriella rolled her eyes and smiled back. "That's fine. I'm holding out for a deal with the Celtics anyway," she joked.

"Thata' girl!" Martha called.

Kelsi laughed as Martha retrieved the ball from the floor and tossed it to Chad, who caught it easily and spun it on one finger.

Troy grabbed it from him. "Leave her alone, guys," he said with a slight frown. "Gabriella might not be Shaq, but not everyone has to be an athlete. She has plenty of other talents."

"Thanks, Troy," Gabriella replied. Still, she couldn't help being a tiny bit insulted. Not an athlete? All she had done was miss one pass. She wasn't *that* uncoordinated! But she didn't say anything. After all, she knew that Troy meant well.

Besides, she was distracted by a commotion from the far end of the hall. Sharpay Evans was coming around the corner with her twin brother, Ryan. Sharpay liked to create a scene wherever she went, but she seemed particularly loud today.

The others noticed, too. "What's up with Sharpay?" Jason wondered.

Chad shrugged. "Noisy...a crowd following her...looks like business as usual to me," he commented.

Gabriella sighed. Sharpay was a talented

actress and the copresident of the East High Drama Club (along with Ryan, of course). But playing the lead role in almost every play or musical wasn't enough for her. She was the kind of person who always acted as if she were performing onstage, even if she was just walking down the hall.

As Sharpay drew closer, Gabriella and her friends could overhear what she was saying. In fact, it was hard *not* to hear it. Ms Darbus, the head of the Drama Club, always liked to tell her young actors to "project, project, PROJECT!" Sharpay definitely had a talent for projecting.

". . . And so now, Daddy is flying the whole family out to L.A. for the premiere," Sharpay was saying to the small but adoring crowd gathered around her. "It's going to be fabulous. We'll probably spend the whole week at our beach house in Malibu – I'm sure half of Hollywood will want to stop by and congratulate us. Not just anyone will be invited to the big night, you know."

"That's right!" Ryan added eagerly. "It's going to be *very* exclusive."

Gabriella couldn't help being curious. "Hi, guys," she said, stepping toward Sharpay and Ryan. "What's going on?"

Chad visibly winced. "Ooh, now she's done it," he muttered, clutching his basketball in both hands. "We're actually going to have to hear about it!"

Sharpay ignored him, even though his comment had been loud enough for her to hear. "Well, I suppose *everyone* will know soon," she told Gabriella. "You may have already heard that my father helped produce a very prestigious independent film this year."

As a matter of fact, Gabriella *hadn't* heard that. Judging by the looks on her friends' faces, neither had they. But it didn't matter. Sharpay didn't wait for a response.

"It's called *Angst in Altoona* and it's had a lot of pre-release buzz," Sharpay said. "In the industry, that's what we say when people are saying positive things about your film before it premieres."

"*We*?" Chad echoed, raising an eyebrow at

Troy and Taylor. Troy shrugged and Taylor just snorted.

"*Angst in Altoona?*" Zeke wrinkled his nose, looking confused.

"Sounds kind of, um, unusual," Martha added.

"Is that Altoona, Pennsylvania?" Jason asked. "Because they have a minor league baseball team – the Curve." Jason knew just about everything there was to know about sports. "Is the movie about baseball?"

"Oh, that'd be cool!" Suddenly, Chad looked a lot more interested. "If it is, can your dad get us free tickets, Sharpay?"

Sharpay rolled her eyes upward. "First of all, it's definitely *not* about baseball," she huffed. "And even if it were, it's not like it's going to be playing at the multiplex down at the mall. This is an *art* film."

"But tell them the best part!" Ryan broke in, practically jumping up and down.

"I'm getting there." Sharpay smoothed down her blond hair. "Daddy is so pleased that he's flying the whole family out to L.A. for the premiere! We'll be staying all week, rubbing elbows with the rich and famous. Isn't that fabulous?"

The gang exchanged surprised looks. This *was* big news!

Sharpay's upcoming trip to L.A. was the talk of East High for the rest of the day. It wasn't often that someone from East High went to Hollywood for a movie premiere.

"It stinks," Chad grumbled, dribbling his basketball down the hall as he and Troy headed for their lockers after last period. Sharpay was just ahead of them, walking in the centre of a small circle of admirers. "Here I was, all psyched about having four days off from school," Chad continued. "And now all I'll be able to think about is how Sharpay and Ryan are spending the week living it up celeb-style!"

"Aw, come on," Troy said. "Honestly, would you want to be going to some Hollywood film premiere? I mean, they'd probably make you wear a suit or something."

Chad scowled. "Hey, bro, for a week living the life in Cali, I'd put on *two* suits."

There was no basketball practice that day, so Troy and Chad headed outside after a quick stop at their lockers. Zeke and Jason were already hanging out on the steps with Martha, Taylor and Kelsi. Chad joined them, while Troy looked around for Gabriella. He wanted to ask her what she had planned for their days off next week. Even though he'd definitely be playing basketball every day, he also wanted to make plans with Gabriella.

He spotted her at the bottom of the steps. "Hi," he said, hurrying over.

"Hi," she replied with a smile.

Before either of them could say anything else, a sleek black sports car pulled up to the curb. The driver honked the horn loudly.

Gabriella shaded her eyes and squinted. "Isn't that Mr Evans's car?"

"Uh-huh," Troy said. He and most of his friends had spent the previous summer working at the nearby Lava Springs Country Club, which meant he'd seen Mr and Mrs Evans pull up in that car more times than he could count.

The door of the black car opened, and Mr Evans got out. He was a handsome, confident looking man. He was wearing a fancy suit and well-polished shoes. He gave the group a friendly wave and started to walk over to them.

"Troy Bolton!" Mr Evans called out in his jovial voice. His white teeth gleamed brightly. "And is that the lovely Gabriella? Nice to see you kids again."

"You too, sir," Troy said with a smile. When Troy was working at the country club, Mr Evans had introduced Troy to some very important people who could help him get on a college basketball team. While that had caused Troy a few problems at the time, he had still appreciated it.

"I hear congratulations are in order," Troy commented to Mr Evans. "Sharpay says your film is going to be a big hit."

Mr Evans chuckled. "Let's hope so," he said. "I didn't get into this venture expecting to make much money, but hey – if it happens, I won't complain!"

At that moment, Sharpay hurried over, with Ryan right at her heels. "What are you doing here, Daddy?" she demanded. "I thought Mother was picking us up and taking us shopping for outfits for the premiere."

"She got held up at her yoga class, princess." Mr Evans said, checking his watch. "I'm going to drop you kids off at the boutique on my way to the office, and she'll join you there in a little while."

Troy and Gabriella's friends had all drifted over to them by now. "That movie premiere sounds awesome, sir," Zeke spoke up.

"Oh, it should be a good time," Mr Evans agreed. Just then, his eyes lit up. "Say, that gives me a terrific idea. Why don't you all come along?"

"*All?*" Sharpay repeated in horror.

"You mean to the movie premiere?" Taylor asked incredulously.

"In *California*?" added Kelsi.

"Really?" Zeke gasped.

"Do we have to wear suits?" asked Chad.

"You can wear whatever you like!" Mr Evans slung an arm around Troy's shoulders and beamed at all of them. "The more the merrier, eh, gang? There's plenty of room at our beach house, and I have more frequent-flier miles than I could ever possibly use, and heck, it's my movie – I should certainly be able to score some extra passes for the premiere. So what do you say?"

"What do we say?" Chad responded for all of them with a grin, pumping his fist in the air. "We say we're going to *Hollywood*!"

CHAPTER TWO

"**W**hoa! This is going to be huge!" Troy exclaimed, after Mr Evans, Sharpay and Ryan had driven away.

"Not just huge," Chad corrected. "It's going to be *epic*." He traded a high five with Jason.

Zeke gave Chad a playful shove. "You'd just better hope your folks let you go. Aren't you grounded because of your low grade on that history test last week? Told ya you should've studied."

Chad gave him an exasperated look. "Details, details. No way will my parents say no to this!"

Gabriella grinned as she and the other girls watched the guys goof around. "That was really generous of Mr Evans to invite us all along."

"I can't believe it!" Martha squealed.

"And to think I was planning to spend next week alphabetizing my sheet music," Kelsi said with a smile.

"Yeah. Taylor and I were going to get a jump start on some term papers," Gabriella said, and glanced over at her friend. But to her surprise, Taylor didn't look excited about the trip at all. She had turned away from the others and was rummaging through her backpack with a grim look on her face.

"Hey, what's wrong?" Gabriella asked.

"Nothing." Taylor didn't meet her eye. "I just don't see the big deal. I mean, sure, it's a free trip to L.A. But is it worth it if we have to spend the whole week listening to Sharpay brag?"

Gabriella was surprised. Taylor and Sharpay didn't always see eye to eye, but they seemed to get along fine – at least most of the time.

"Oh, come on," Gabriella replied. "She's not

that bad."

"And Ryan's cool, right?" Kelsi spoke up.

"Right!" Martha exclaimed. "Remember how much fun we had working with him on the talent show over the summer?"

"I bet we'll all have a blast next week," Gabriella said.

Taylor slung her bag over her shoulder. "Excuse me. I'm going to miss my bus." She spun on her heel and marched off down the sidewalk.

Gabriella hurried after Taylor, catching up with her near the bus lot. "Hey! Want to tell me what's going on?" She gave Taylor a friendly smile.

Taylor turned to face her. She glanced around and saw that nobody else was close enough to overhear them. Then she sighed and tugged on her glossy black hair. "It's just...I'm not sure I'll be allowed to go."

"What?" Gabriella blinked. "Why not?"

Taylor shook her head. "My parents might seem normal on the outside, but there are things you don't know about them, Gabriella. For instance, they practically freak out anytime I want to go to a sleepover at a friend's house. And that's just for one night. It took me weeks to convince them to let me go to New York City for the *College Quizmaster* show, and I don't even want to admit how long I had to work on them before they agreed to our New Year's ski trip. They'll never in a million years let me just jet off to California," she said sadly.

Gabriella bit her lip. She didn't like seeing her friend so upset, and she certainly didn't want Taylor to have to miss all the fun. The trip wouldn't be the same if she couldn't go.

"Well, all you can do is ask, right?" Gabriella asked hopefully. "Maybe they'll surprise you. I mean, you're a senior now. Just remind them that in another year, they're going to have to let you leave home to go off to college."

"Yeah, if I'm lucky," Taylor muttered. "Maybe they'll make me commute to college right here in Albuquerque, and I'll have to live at home forever." She sighed. "But I guess you're right, Gabriella. I can ask."

"I *cannot* believe you asked all those random people to come along on our L.A. trip!" Sharpay fumed from the backseat of her father's car. She drummed her manicured fingernails angrily on her armrest.

Mr Evans glanced over, one eyebrow raised in surprise. "They're not random people, princess," he said. "They're your friends and classmates. I thought it would be fun to have them along."

Ryan nodded. "Chill out, sis."

"Chill out? *Chill out?*" Sharpay glared at her brother. "Don't tell me to chill out! I —"

"Here we are!" her father interrupted, sounding relieved. He pulled in front of one of the city's most exclusive clothing boutiques. "Your mother will be along soon."

Sharpay flung open the car door, climbed out, and stomped across the pavment. Ryan ran after her.

"Look, what's the big deal?" he asked as they entered the boutique. The smell of roses hung in the air. "Dad's right. Those *random people are* our friends. It'll be fun to have them come to our beach house."

"Get real, Ryan!" Sharpay exclaimed so loudly that the well-dressed saleswoman at the counter looked up with a scowl. Sharpay yanked her brother behind an evening-wear rack and continued in a lower voice, "This trip isn't just about the premiere."

"Sharpay, what are you talking about?" Ryan asked, reaching out to touch the sleeve of a velvet jacket.

Sharpay sighed in frustration. "Pay attention, Ryan!" she commanded. He looked back at her.

"The thing is, I figure this trip could be my big break if I play it right," Sharpay said with a mischievous smile. Her eyes took on a faraway look. "Daddy's connections should open some doors for me next week. A few visits to some studio lots, a few meetings with casting agents, and *voila*! I'll be Hollywood's next rising star." Grabbing a feather boa off one of the dresses hanging in front of them, she slung it around her neck and posed like a model.

"O-*kay*," Ryan said slowly. "But what difference does it make if our friends come? Actually, I'm surprised you're not more excited that Zeke Baylor will be walking down a red carpet with you," he said with a small smirk.

Sharpay blushed. Ever since the Wildcats' ski trip over New Year's break, when Zeke revealed that he was the one who had sent the search party to rescue her after she got stranded in the woods, they'd shared a special bond. She took a deep breath and quickly refocused, back to the topic at hand.

"I'm not looking for fun, Ryan!" she raised her voice again and tossed the feather boa back onto the rack. "I'm really going to get myself *discovered*...and I don't need a bunch of amateurs getting in my way."

"Okay." Ryan leaned closer and smiled. "But think about it, Sharpay. Won't your triumph be that much sweeter with all those witnesses?"

"Hmm." Sharpay rubbed her chin thoughtfully. "Maybe you *do* have a point there...."

"Hello, my darlings!" Their mother's cheerful voice broke in. Mrs Evans hurried up to them, looking perfectly put together, as usual. "I hope you haven't been waiting long. By the way, your father called and told me about inviting all your school friends along on our L.A. trip. Do you think we should pick up some outfits for opening night for them, too? I doubt most of them have anything suitable. Do they?"

"Excellent point, Mother." Sharpay smirked. "In fact, I'm sure *most* of them aren't prepared for this trip in a lot of ways. Maybe we'd better make sure they sit in coach on the flight out. We wouldn't want to overwhelm anyone, would we?"

* * *

"Gabriella? Earth to Gabriella!" Troy waved a hand in front of her face.

"Hmm?" Gabriella blinked and looked up at him. "Oh! Sorry, Troy. Was I doing it again?"

He sighed and looked at Gabriella curiously. It was Saturday night, and they were sitting in a booth at their favourite restaurant. But Gabriella had hardly touched her burger or said a word since they'd arrived. Troy knew the reason – she was distracted because they still didn't know whether Taylor was going to be able to come along to California. Everyone else had already received permission – even Chad's parents had agreed he could go, as long as he promised to ask his history teacher for extra help so he could bring his grade up.

But Taylor's parents still hadn't made a decision. They hadn't said no when she'd asked them, but they hadn't exactly said yes, either.

"I just wish there was something we could do to help," Gabriella murmured, picking at her food.

"I know what you mean," Troy said. He leaned his elbows on the table. "I feel like calling up Taylor's folks and begging them to let her go. Unfortunately, I don't think they care what I..." His voice trailed off as an idea popped into his head. "Wait!" he blurted out. "Taylor's parents might not care what *I* think. But there's someone who might be a little more convincing."

Gabriella tilted her head, looking confused.

"Who?"

"Hang on a sec." Troy grinned and pulled out his mobile phone. He dialed, then put it to his ear and waited. "Hello, Mr Evans?" he said when a voice answered. "This is Troy Bolton....Good to talk to you, too, sir!" He winked at Gabriella. "Listen, I know it's a lot to ask, but do you think you could do me a favour...?"

CHAPTER THREE

"**C**heck it out! I see a palm tree!" Chad exclaimed, his face pressed up against the airplane window. It was early Tuesday morning, and their plane had just landed at the airport in California.

Zeke leaned forward and then rolled his eyes. "Big deal," he said. "My mum has a palm tree growing in her garden at home."

"Yeah, but this is an *L.A.* palm tree," Chad replied. "*Totally* different thing!"

"Sit down and fasten your seat belt," Taylor

24

ordered, pulling Chad back into the seat beside her. "The captain doesn't turn off the safety-belt sign until the plane docks at the terminal."

Gabriella was sitting in the aisle seat on Taylor's other side. She smiled to herself. She could hardly believe they were here – *all* of them. Luckily, Troy's idea had done the trick. Mr Evans called Taylor's parents and convinced them to let her come along.

Gabriella glanced around the crowded plane. Martha, Jason, Zeke and Kelsi were in the row behind her. Troy was sitting right across the aisle from her. He met her eyes as she looked toward him.

"This is great, isn't it?" he asked, reaching across the aisle to take her hand.

"Sure is!" Jason called out, leaning forward. "Too bad only Sharpay and Ryan get to sit with their parents in first class, though."

"That's okay." Chad grinned. "I'd sit on the wing if I had to!"

Once the plane docked, the group found the Evans family waiting for them on the enclosed ramp leading from the plane into the airport. "Everyone have a nice flight?" Mrs Evans asked. "I thought the complimentary hot towels were a lovely touch, didn't you?"

"Hot towels?" Chad repeated. "What hot towels?"

Sharpay didn't wait for anyone else to answer. "Hurry up!" she ordered, speeding ahead of the group. "We're on a tight schedule."

Sharpay was walking so fast that the others had trouble keeping up. When she reached the door leading into the airport, she suddenly stopped short. Ryan almost bumped into her.

"Hold this," Sharpay told him, shrugging off the jacket she'd been wearing on the plane. Underneath, she was dressed in a shimmering gold halter top and white satin trousers. Gabriella's eyes widened as she took in Sharpay's outfit. It certainly made Gabriella's own jeans and red T-shirt look kind of shabby.

"Looks like someone's ready to hit the hip-hop clubs," Martha said.

"Whoa," Zeke commented. "Nice outfit, Sharpay."

"It's fabulous, isn't it?" She pushed through the door and swept out into the waiting area. To her gratification, several people immediately turned to stare. One even grabbed his camera and snapped her photo.

"Who is that?" a young girl asked her friend in a loud whisper. "Is she someone famous?"

The other girl shrugged. "I don't know. Maybe!"

"No autographs, please!" Sharpay called out as she strode across the waiting room. She smiled, pausing and striking a pose as several other people took her picture. Being a Hollywood star was going to be a snap, Sharpay thought. She was already a natural!

"I can't believe we're really here," Kelsi said, her eyes wide. The whole group was on a spacious deck overlooking the Pacific Ocean. Everyone was enjoying the lavish buffet-style lunch that had been waiting for them upon their arrival at the Evans's Malibu beach house half an hour earlier.

"I feel kind of like we're all starring in an episode of *Malibu Prep*," Martha joked.

"Oh, I *love* that show!" Gabriella exclaimed.

Zeke was staring through the French doors and looking at the tasteful interior of the Evans's house. "This place is incredible," he said.

Mr Evans smiled. "Oh, it's not much," he said modestly. "But we do enjoy it. As I said before, please make yourselves at home."

"But not *too* much at home," Sharpay warned. "Everyone needs to finish eating quickly. Our tour of the stars' homes and then of Hollywood starts in exactly twenty minutes."

"Tour?" Chad looked up from his smoked turkey and Brie sandwich. "Thanks, but I think I'll pass. I was planning to hit the beach right after lunch."

Gabriella nodded. "I thought it might be nice to just lie by the pool and relax for a while, if that's okay," she said.

"Did you guys see the game room in the basement?" Jason's eyes sparkled. "We have *got* to try out that vintage pinball machine!"

Sharpay groaned. "No!" she exclaimed sharply. "You guys can goof off later. Daddy went to a lot of trouble to set up this tour for us."

"It's okay, princess," Mr Evans said. "If they want to stick around and enjoy the house and beach today, we can reschedule the tour for later in the week."

Sharpay frowned. What was the big deal about their beach house, anyway? It was just a house – not even anywhere near as nice as their home back in Albuquerque. And the beach would be there all week.

"I won't hear of it, Daddy," she insisted, glaring at the others. "We totally appreciate you going to so much trouble."

"Er, that's right, sir," Troy said, shooting a look at his friends. "We appreciate everything you've done to make this trip happen. We'd love to check it out, wouldn't we, guys?"

The others agreed, some with more enthusiasm than others. But Sharpay didn't care what they thought, as long as they went along with her plans. She had this whole week scheduled down to the minute, and the Hollywood tour was going to be the big kickoff.

Naturally, Sharpay was already quite familiar with L.A. She and Ryan had visited many times with their parents, but she figured the tour would be a nice, welcome-back treat for herself. After all, she knew she'd be spending most of the rest of the week in important meetings and auditions. What could possibly psych her up more than seeing celebrities' homes and getting a refresher tour of the city?

Later that night, the whole group was having dinner at a Chinese restaurant near Hollywood. Gabriella was sitting beside Troy, and the rest of their friends were all around them. Mrs Evans was sitting at the far end of the table, while Mr Evans had wandered off to talk with a bunch of men in business suits in the lounge. Before he'd gone, though, he'd told all the kids to order whatever they liked.

Troy was having an awesome time so far.

They'd had a tour bus all to themselves that afternoon – just as Sharpay had promised. The guide had showed them all around Hollywood. At one point, they even got an up-close look at the stars' handprints in the sidewalk in front of Grauman's Chinese Theatre. The driver had taken them past the homes of various celebrities in Beverly Hills and other exclusive areas. The guide told them lots of fun stories about the stars and their neighbourhoods and houses.

"How cool was it to see where Anne Hathaway lives?" Gabriella asked, reaching out to help herself to more stir-fried vegetables. "I love her!"

"Me, too," Martha agreed.

"And what did you think of George Gershwin's house?" Kelsi gushed. "I was – oh, my gosh!" She gasped, interrupting herself. "Look over there! Isn't that Melody Swanson?"

A gorgeous woman with blond hair had just walked into the restaurant, accompanied by several other people. Troy's eyes widened as he recognized the actress. She had starred in dozens of movies over the past decade.

"It *is* her!" Gabriella exclaimed, clutching Troy's arm.

"She looks just like she does in the movies!" Taylor gasped.

"Who did you expect her to look like? Godzilla?" Chad joked. But he also looked a bit in awe as he stared at the famous actress.

Sharpay was sitting a few seats down, between her mother and Ryan. She suddenly noticed the commotion at the other end of the table.

"What are you guys talking about?" She followed their gaze and spotted Melody Swanson. For a second, she was impressed. But she shook it off immediately. "Oh, right," she said with a casual shrug. "Well, that's Hollywood – we spot a star or two almost every time we come out here. Isn't that right, Mother?"

"That's true, dear," her mother said with a serene smile.

Taylor was rummaging through her purse. "Who has a pen?" she asked. "I want to go ask for her autograph."

"No!" Sharpay exclaimed, mortified. "You

can't bother her. Do you want to look like some small-town tourist?"

Chad shrugged. "If the small-town shoe fits, I say, wear it," he said, grabbing the pen Taylor had just found. "Come on! Let's go say hi."

"Wait!" Sharpay cried. "At least show some manners...."

But nobody was listening. Sharpay shuddered as she watched them stampede toward the actress's table.

"Want to go with them?" Ryan suggested to his mother eagerly.

"Go ahead," his mother urged, taking a sip of her green tea. "Get an autograph for me, too."

"Stop!" Sharpay barked. She grabbed her brother before he could stand up. On the one hand, she wanted to play it cool. But it seemed a little late for that, considering that her class-mates were already surrounding the actress. If she couldn't beat them, she supposed she might as well join them.

"Uh, I mean, wait for me," she told Ryan, sounding a little kinder. "I suppose I should at least go apologize to Ms Swanson for how those *amateurs* are mobbing her."

She hurried over and pushed her way to the front of the crowd. The actress's smile stretched from ear to ear as she signed the side of Chad's basketball shoe.

"Sorry it's a little stinky," Chad said with a grin. "I didn't know it would be getting this close to a celebrity's nose."

"It's quite all right." Melody chuckled and handed back the shoe. "Anything for a fan."

"*Excuse* me." Sharpay pushed past Kelsi, Martha and Taylor. "Ms Swanson, I'm Sharpay Evans. I'm an actress myself."

"Is that so? Marvellous," the actress replied, smiling. "Would you like an autograph, sweetie?"

"Actually, what I'd like is some advice." Sharpay shot Melody her most winning smile. "Who's your agent? Oh, and if you have his cell number and e-mail address handy, I could use those, too."

"Er..." Melody looked taken aback.

"Oh!" Sharpay continued. "Also, I heard

you're playing Joan of Arc in an upcoming mini-series. Do you by any chance need a talented blond stand-in for any of your close-ups?" She smoothed down her golden hair and struck a regal pose.

"I don't think so," Melody answered and checked her watch. "I'm afraid you'll all have to excuse me. I just remembered I have an appointment. Right now."

She and her companions stood up. Before Sharpay could protest, they quickly walked toward the exit.

"Why, Sharpay," Chad commented, "I thought all this Hollywood stuff was old news to you? You were, well..."

"Pushy? Obnoxious?" Taylor chimed in.

Sharpay shrugged them off. "Whatever," she replied blithely. "I'm sure Melody understood where I was coming from. She's been there her-self – a long time ago, but still..." She tilted her head thoughtfully. "Come to think of it, she might have been a little threatened by me."

"By you?" Gabriella blinked. "Um..."

Sharpay sighed. "Actresses can *always* spot talent. She was probably afraid that if I showed up on the set as her Joan of Arc stand-in, I'd end up stealing the part from her." Sharpay shrugged. "Can't blame her for that. I mean, she *is* right."

The others exchanged dubious glances. But Sharpay didn't mind. They just didn't understand. If you wanted to make it in Hollywood, you had to be willing to do whatever it took.

CHAPTER FOUR

The next morning, Sharpay climbed out of a taxi in front of a big movie studio.

"Come on, Ryan," Sharpay said as she smoothed down a small wrinkle in her crisp linen pants. "Let's go make me a star!"

Ryan stifled a yawn as he got out of the car after her. He glanced up at the impressive-looking studio gates in front of them. It was very early, and he thought longingly of the rest of the gang, still blissfully sleeping back at the beach house. Lucky them. But he had known better than to suggest to Sharpay that they get started a little later.

"So, when's your first appointment?" he asked sleepily.

Sharpay shrugged. "Oh, I ended up deciding just to wing it today," she replied with an airy wave. "There wasn't enough time for all the producers and agents I called to get back to me before we left home, so I couldn't set up any official meetings. But I'm sure they can squeeze me in, now that I'm here."

She hurried forward, eager to start making her Hollywood dreams come true. But she almost immediately found her path blocked by the studio gate. A stout, middle-aged man wearing a uniform was sitting on a stool beside it.

"Pass, please," he said in a bored-sounding voice, barely looking up from his crossword puzzle.

"Yes, that's right," Sharpay responded impatiently. "We'd like to *pass*, please. Could you open this gate?"

The man glanced up, clearly irritated. "No, I need to see your *pass*, please," he replied. "That's what makes me open the gate."

Sharpay cleared her throat, slightly annoyed. "I don't think you understand. I'm Sharpay Evans," she said. "My father is Vance Evans, the *highly* respected film producer."

"Sorry," the guard retorted. He had already returned his attention to his puzzle, and this time he didn't look up at all. "No pass, no entry. Those are the rules."

"What?" Sharpay crossed her arms over her chest. Her cheerful mood was now completely clouded over by the guard's ignorance. "You *must* be kidding me. Haven't you ever heard of *Angst in Altoona*?"

"Nope. But I've heard of *Bothered in Burbank*." The guard glanced up as a man dressed in khakis and worn-out sneakers walked briskly toward them. Hopping off his stool with a polite nod, the guard opened the gate just wide enough to let the man through.

"Hey!" Sharpay protested. "*He* didn't show a

pass, and you let him through!"

"*He* runs Top Drawer Pictures." The guard sat back down on his stool and picked up his puzzle. "When you can say the same, blondie, come on back and we'll talk."

"Ooh!" Sharpay stomped her foot. She was so frustrated that, for once, she was at a loss for words.

"Come on, sis," Ryan said. "Maybe we should try somewhere else."

Sharpay grabbed her mobile phone out of her purse. "Not so fast," she snipped. "I'm calling Daddy. He'll straighten things out."

A few moments later, one of her father's friends was on the phone with the guard, explaining the situation.

"All right, sir," the guard dubiously said into the phone, eyeing Sharpay suspiciously. "Yeah, I suppose they look harmless enough....Okay. Good-bye." He hung up and stepped toward the gate. "Okay. You can go in."

"That's more like it!" Sharpay cried. She tilted her nose upward and strutted through the open gate.

Ryan smiled sheepishly at the guard as he scurried after her. "Thanks," he told the guard. "Good luck with your crosswords."

The guard just grunted in response. Then he swung the gate shut behind them with a loud clang.

Back in Malibu, Troy and Gabriella headed down the wooden steps leading from the Evans's house to the beach. "It's so beautiful here!" Gabriella exclaimed, pausing to survey the scene.

The late-morning sun reflected off the waves. A few people were jogging along the shoreline, and an excited dog frolicked in the surf near its owner. It looked a little more crowded further down the beach, but here they had the place almost to themselves.

"Definitely," Troy agreed, reaching for her hand and giving it a light squeeze. "I could get used to this California lifestyle."

"I know," said Gabriella. "Could you believe some of those gorgeous houses we saw on the tour yesterday?"

The two of them stepped down onto the warm sand and started wandering along the beach.

"I have to say, I wasn't too psyched about the tour when Sharpay started bossing us around about going," Troy admitted. "But in the end, it was fun."

"That movie premiere on Saturday night should be fun, too," Gabriella added. She shivered with anticipation. "Just think – us, rubbing shoulders with Hollywood's elite. Sort of like seeing Melody Swanson last night, only even better!"

"Uh-huh." Troy was staring straight ahead.

Gabriella glanced over at him. "Troy?" she asked. "What's wrong?"

"Check it out." Troy pointed at three surfers riding some waves in the distance. "Look at their moves! And they don't even look much older than us."

Gabriella watched as the three surfers zipped along effortlessly. "Wow," she marvelled. "They're good!"

"*Really* good," Troy agreed. He stared admiringly as one of the two male surfers did an expert cutback. "I'd love to learn to do that!"

"Me, too," Gabriella said.

Troy shot her a glance. "You *would*?" he asked.

She raised an eyebrow at him. "Yes, I would," she responded coolly. "Why?"

"I mean, that's great," Troy quickly said. "I'm just surprised....It looks pretty tricky."

Gabriella bit her lip. She was so used to Troy supporting her that she just hadn't expected him to look at her as if she had no athletic abilities whatsoever. Did he forget that she had spent last summer as a lifeguard?

But she didn't say anything more, and Troy had already returned to watching the surfers. Besides, she didn't want to argue over something so silly. It was just an innocent comment, after all.

"They've definitely got talent," Gabriella commented, changing the subject. "Let's go meet them!"

By the time Troy and Gabriella got there, all

three of the surfers had just reached the beach.

"Hi," the female surfer greeted them. She had a freckled face and a friendly smile. "Haven't seen you two around here before. You staying nearby?"

"Yep," Troy replied. "We're staying with a friend for the week. Right over there." He pointed out the Evans's beach house.

"Nice," one of the male surfers said. "Welcome to Malibu, dudes!"

Troy and Gabriella were still chatting with the friendly trio a few minutes later when Jason and Zeke headed over to them.

"Hey!" Jason exclaimed, his eyes widening. "I can't believe it. Look who it is!"

Troy laughed. "Did you miss me that much since I saw you, like, five minutes ago?" he teased. "Seriously, though. You two should see these guys surf. They've got some amazing moves."

"Yeah, no kidding," Jason said. He was staring at the surfers in awe. "Don't tell me you don't recognize them, Bolton! They're Trish Waverly, Bob 'Banzai' Santos and Louie Kelly!

44

They're champion surfers!"

Gabriella knew that Jason was practically a walking sports encyclopedia. Still, she was kind of impressed that he'd recognized the trio.

"Awesome to meet you, dude." Louie offered Jason his hand. "I'm always stoked to run into a fan."

Soon all seven of them had traded introductions. "I still can't believe this," Jason said, grinning with excitement. "It must be so great to just travel around surfing all the best beaches!"

"It's pretty rad," Banzai admitted. "We're lucky."

"Definitely," Trish said. "We're just happy to be able to make a living doing something we love."

"Any of you ever been on a board before?" Louie asked.

The East High students shook their heads.

"Only on the snow," Troy said.

"I tried once, but totally wiped out," Jason admitted. "So that doesn't really count."

"Want to give it a try?" Banzai asked, giving

the students a wide grin. "We've got some extra boards in the car."

"Wait!" Zeke exclaimed. "You're going to teach us to surf?"

"Sure, if you're up for it," Louie replied.

"Sweet!" Jason cried, trading a high five with Zeke.

Trish laughed. "Guess we'll take that as a yes."

"What about the others?" Gabriella asked, realizing that Chad, Taylor, Martha and Kelsi were about to miss out on an awesome experience. She quickly explained the situation to the famous surfers.

"What are you waiting for?" Banzai asked Gabriella. "Go get 'em! And let's get shredding!"

Gabriella giggled. She wasn't sure exactly what "shredding" meant, but it sounded like fun. "Be right back," she said and took off for the house. She couldn't wait to give surfing a try. How hard could it be?

CHAPTER FIVE

Meanwhile, back at the studio, Sharpay wasn't having much luck jump-starting her fabulous career. She and Ryan had been hanging out at the movie lot all morning, but nobody had given them the time of day.

"This is ridiculous," she muttered, stalking down a beige-carpeted hallway in one of the studio's office buildings. "Can't these people even recognize huge potential when it's standing right in front of them?"

Ryan shrugged. "Maybe you'd be better off

making some appointments. I mean, an awful lot of people seem to be late for appointments when we try to talk to them." He smiled hopefully. "Maybe if we went back to the beach house and made a few calls, you could *be* one of those appointments! You could do your thing and still get in some beach time with the gang."

"Don't be silly, Ryan." At the moment, Sharpay didn't have time to explain in detail all the ways he was completely wrong. "We're here *now*. I'm going to get someone to take me seriously, even if I have to knock on every single door in this place!"

With that, she lifted her hand to knock on yet another random door. It was only then that she noticed the brass name plate on the next door down. She gasped, her fist frozen in midair.

"Do you see that?" she asked increduously. "Michael Torrent! He's the hottest young director in Hollywood today – he directed *Playing with Fire!*"

Ryan nodded appreciatively. "That movie rocked."

Sharpay hardly heard him. She smoothed her clothes, ran her hand down the back of her hair, smacked her lips, and rushed over to the door. It was slightly ajar, revealing a slim, rumple-haired young man. He was seated at a desk, hunched over a computer.

Sharpay was surprised to see that he was dressed in baggy shorts and a T-shirt with what appeared to be a big coffee stain on the front. But she shrugged it off. That was Hollywood for you. Once you were successful enough, you could be as eccentric – or as fashion unconscious – as you wanted.

"Yoo-hoo!" she called, pushing the door open a bit wider. "Anybody home? Why, Mr Torrent, what an honour," she said, feigning surprise.

The man looked up and blinked at her increduously. "Oh," he said. "I'm – "

She didn't give him a chance to continue. She already knew what he was going to say – *I'm sorry, I'm late for an appointment.* Just like all the others. Well, enough was enough. This time, she wasn't taking no for an answer.

49

"I've seen all of your films," she said, stepping into the office and shooting him her best, thousand-watt superstar smile. "You're definitely my all-time favourite director. And I'm not just saying that as some casual, know-nothing fan, either. I'm an *actress*. Actually, a singer-dancer-actress, if you want to get technical." She laughed modestly.

"Okay," the guy said slowly. "But, listen, I – "

"No, please." Sharpay tried to keep the edge of desperation out of her voice, but it wasn't easy. "You need to listen to me. All I need is one shot, and I can prove to you I've got what it takes. My name is Sharpay Evans. I've been performing since before I could walk. I do tap, ballet, jazz, ballroom, and, um, well – everything, pretty much! I have a three-octave range, just about, and I can act any part there is." She yanked Ryan forward. "This is my brother – he choreographs most of our routines. Although I do provide plenty of input on that, too, of course."

She cleared her throat. Normally she would never even consider performing without a proper warm-up. But this was an extremely unique situation.

"Ready, Ryan?" she said brightly. " 'Bop to the Top,' from the top. One, two, three . . ."

Ryan was a little slow on the uptake. He just stared at her as she danced the first few steps. Luckily, Sharpay had a solo on the first couple of bars of the song, anyway. By the time he was supposed to come in, he had recovered from his initial surprise and joined in, singing and dancing alongside her. They ended their number with a dramatic kneeling pose and jazz hands.

Sharpay gave the man a winning smile. "Okay, so now you see I can sing and dance," she told him. "Bet you can't believe I can do all that and act, too, huh? Well, prepare to be impressed."

She cleared her throat again. Without giving the man a chance to react, she launched into Lady Macbeth's soliloquy from *Macbeth*. She put every bit of thespian skill she possessed into the part, acting so dramatically that she almost knocked over a large picture frame. Luckily,

Ryan caught it just before it hit the floor.

When she finished, Sharpay bowed deeply. The guy at the desk clapped enthusiastically.

"Wow," he remarked. "You're terrific!"

"Thank you!" Sharpay gave him a small curtsy. *Now* she was getting somewhere! All the brush-offs, the slammed doors, and the rude assistants had been worth it.

"So, what do you say?" she asked, leaning across the desk with a satisfied grin. "Is there a part in your next picture for a girl like me? I wouldn't even have to start with the lead role. Just a majour supporting character would be fine."

"Um, not exactly." The guy shrugged. "See, I was trying to tell you earlier. I'm not Michael Torrent."

"You're not?" Sharpay blinked. Was this some kind of weird Hollywood humor?

"Nope. I'm Carl. The computer-tech guy. Mr Torrent's hard drive is on the blink." He waved a hand at the computer and smiled sheepishly. "Hey, but I bet Mr Torrent would love to meet you when he gets back from New York next week."

"Oh." Sharpay could feel her throat tightening. She spun on her heel and stormed out of the office. Ryan gave Carl a polite nod and followed after her.

Back at the beach, the rest of the Wildcats were having an awesome time learning how to surf.

"Wipeout!" Chad cried. He popped up from beneath the wave that had just knocked him off his board. His curly hair was plastered to his head.

Troy laughed. "Way to ride the wave, dude!" he called. He glanced over at Louie, who was standing on the sand beside him. "So, would you show me the right way to stand up on the board again? I want to do a little better than my friend out there."

"Sure, man," Louie said. He flopped down onto Troy's board, which was lying at the edge of the water. "Okay, so you start out like this, right. Then you want to..."

Louie kept talking, but Troy wasn't paying attention. He'd just spotted Gabriella splashing out through the breakers beside Zeke, Martha, and Trish. All of them were carrying surfboards.

Troy frowned slightly as he watched. He was having a fantastic time learning to surf from the three young champs, but he just couldn't stop worrying about Gabriella. At first he'd assumed she would hang back – maybe do a little bodysurfing in the shallows. But she kept insisting on learning the real moves. The trouble was, she wasn't used to that kind of rough-and-tumble workout. He was afraid she would get hurt if she wasn't careful.

"Hey, Gabriella!" he called. "Want to take a break and go grab a lemonade or something?"

"Not right now!" she shouted back. "Trish thinks I'm ready to try standing up on the board!"

"A pop-up," Trish added. "That's what it's called, remember?"

"Go for it!" Louie yelled, giving her an enthusiastic thumbs-up.

Gabriella grinned and returned the gesture. She turned and paddled out after Trish, Martha, and Zeke.

Troy bit his lip. He was tempted to swim out after Gabriella and try to talk her out of it. What if she slipped and hit her head on her surfboard?

He watched nervously as she caught a wave. For a second, it looked like she was getting the hang of it! He started to smile with relief.

But then Gabriella started to wobble uncontrollably, and her surfboard shot out from under her. She tumbled backward off her board, splashing into the foam.

"Gabriella!" Troy dropped his surfboard and raced into the water. But he was barely ankle deep when Gabriella popped into view again, laughing as she spit out a mouthful of saltwater. She grabbed her board and bodyboarded in on the remainder of the wave.

Phew! Troy felt himself relax. That had been close.

"Gabriella looks pretty great out there," Chad observed.

Troy glanced at him. He hadn't even realized Chad had come up beside him until he spoke.

"Yeah," Troy said grimly. "So great I've got 9-1-1 on speed dial."

Chad shot him a surprised look. "Chill, bro," he told Troy. "She's just having a good time like the rest of us."

Troy nodded hesitantly. Part of him knew that his friend was right. But another part couldn't help worrying anyway.

By now Gabriella was splashing toward him through the shallows. "Did you see me?" she asked him with a grin. "I totally wiped out."

"I saw." Troy forced a smile. "Listen, maybe you should take a break before you push it too far and get hurt or something. How about we go grab that lemonade?"

"No way," she said, shaking her head. "I almost had it. I just need to catch my breath for a sec, and then I'm going to give it another try."

"Are you sure?" Troy asked with concern.

"I'm sure." She shot him an annoyed look.

"After all, why should only the *athletes* have all the fun?"

Troy wasn't sure what she meant by that. And she didn't give him a chance to ask. Zeke and Martha had just bodyboarded in on another wave, and Gabriella waded off through the surf to join them.

CHAPTER SIX

"**W**hat's *wrong* with everyone in this place?" Sharpay asked, as yet another door slammed in her face. Literally.

She and Ryan had been wandering around the lot for hours, and she was no closer to being discovered than when she'd arrived that morning. The closest she'd come to an audition was her encounter with Carl the computer-tech guy. And *that* certainly wasn't going to get her in front of any cameras.

"Maybe we should head back to the house and regroup," Ryan suggested. "You know — relax on the beach for a while, hang out with our friends..."

"Maybe we should try a different studio," Sharpay shot back and headed for the exit of the building they were in. "*This* one is obviously not the right one."

As she strode across the parking lot, Ryan had to break into a jog to keep up. "Don't worry, Sharpay," he said. "Even the biggest stars talk about having to pay their dues. Well, maybe today is *your* dues."

Sharpay didn't answer. Instead, she tilted her head and stared at a big, warehouse-like building nearby. "Hey, do you hear that?" she asked.

"Hear what?" Ryan cocked his head, too. He couldn't make out any particular sounds, except the faraway noise of a lawn mower.

"It sounds like music," Sharpay commented. "Come on. Let's go see what it is!"

Soon they were peeking in through the door of another studio-lot building. Inside, they saw a huge, cavernous space. People scurried busily back and forth. A few people were pushing large camera equipment around. One area was full of scenery that included a row of lockers and some colourful banners with the name FAIRVIEW HIGH printed on them.

Sharpay gasped. "It's a soundstage!" she whispered to Ryan. "They must be shooting a movie *right now*!" She took in the sights and sounds of more than a dozen dancers and singers warming up nearby. "And it looks like a *musical*! It's perfect!"

Ryan looked over at the singers and dancers in awe. "Hollywood doesn't make nearly enough musicals these days. It's a shame, really, since almost everyone loves..." His voice trailed off when he realized Sharpay wasn't standing next to him anymore. He looked through the door and spotted her making a beeline toward the group. He hurried after her.

"Um, Sharpay? Where are you going?" he asked.

"Sshh!" she hushed him. "Don't you see? This is the big break I've been waiting for! It's a musical set in a high school." She glanced from the locker scenery to the singers and dancers, all of whom were young and dressed like ordinary teenagers.

Ryan blinked. "You mean you're going to find the director and ask if you can be in *this* movie?" he asked incredulously.

Sharpay just smirked. "I'm not going to *ask*, silly," she said. "I'm just going to join the group and let my talent speak for itself. Or, rather, my singing and dancing speak for itself. Anyway, didn't I impress that computer-tech guy?" Without waiting for a response, she sprinted over to the singers and dancers and did her best to act nonchalant. A couple of the dancers shot her curious looks, but she just started doing stretches and acting as if she'd been there all along.

Nearby, a couple of girls were chatting as they warmed up. "So, is Destiny here yet?" one of them asked in a bored voice.

The second girl stopped to adjust her ponytail. "Haven't seen her," she replied. "She'll probably walk in half an hour late, as usual."

The first performer sighed. "Most likely complaining about all the traffic between here and the *TRK* studio."

Sharpay's eyes widened as she realized they were talking about Destiny Phyllips, the star of the hit teen TV drama, *Twin River Knoll*. Destiny must be the star of this film, too! Come to think of it, Sharpay did remember reading something about Destiny being cast in a new movie musical.

Someday that'll be me, Sharpay thought with determination. I'll be the one being gossiped about by a couple of backup dancers!

Just then, there was a commotion at the far end of the soundstage. Sharpay glanced over and saw Destiny hurrying in. She looked a lot shorter in person than she did on TV.

"Sorry I'm late, everyone," she said breezily. "Traffic was just *horrendous*. I can't believe my limo made it!"

The young star was immediately swarmed by a small band of costume and make-up people. She was bustled off the set while everyone else went back to what they'd been doing. Sharpay sneaked a peek at her watch. With any luck, she'd be a movie star before dinnertime!

Finally, Destiny emerged from her dressing room, looking refreshed and relaxed. She wandered over toward the locker-lined set.

"Places, everyone!" shouted a man with a bullhorn. "We're going to start with the 'Detention's Not Fair' number. I want to get it all in one take this time, and we'll go back and fill in the blanks later. From the intro, please."

Sharpay moved toward the set with the others, pretending she knew what she was doing. When the rest of the chorus started milling around in front of the lockers, she took the cue and did her best to blend in near the back. She figured she could move up to a more prominent spot once she'd had a chance to figure out the scene.

Someone turned on the music. The director shouted, "Action!" and the scene began. Destiny sauntered down the "hallway" with two other actresses.

"It's just not fair!" Destiny cried with a pout,

tossing her glossy blond hair over one shoulder. "I can't believe Mr Trenton did this to me. All I did was answer one text during history class. I certainly didn't deserve detention!"

A good-looking guy leaped forward. "Did you say you got detention?" he cried.

All of a sudden, everyone broke into song. The cast traded lyrics back and forth as they sang about the injustice of school detention. The melody was pretty simple – certainly nothing Sharpay couldn't handle. She faked her way along until she picked up enough to feel confident in singing out. As she did, she slowly worked her way toward the front of the group until she was directly behind Destiny Phyllips.

It's working! Sharpay thought. They'll see my face in every shot. As soon as a few casting agents see how I look on film, I'll be offered so many scripts that I'll have to hire someone just to help me read them all.

Destiny sang a few more lines and executed some flashy dance steps. With that, the whole cast started to dance. Sharpay, startled, got bumped by one of the girls she'd overheard talking earlier. The dancer shot her an irritated glare.

Sharpay gulped, doing her best to follow what the others were doing. Two steps left, turn, lunge forward, kick...

But she could only fake her way through the routine for so long. A sudden heel, ball, change took her by surprise. She leaped forward, trying to catch up...just as everyone else spun and stepped back. She ended up accidentally bumping into Destiny and sending her crashing to the floor.

"Hey!" the young star cried. "What are you doing?"

"Sorry!" Sharpay exclaimed, her face bright red. "I'm sooo sorry, Miss Phyllips. I just got the steps mixed up for a second."

"Cut!" The director was striding toward them, glaring. "What's going on here?"

Destiny had scrambled to her feet by now, aided by one of the male dancers. "I'll tell you what's going on!" she exclaimed. "Miss Two Left Feet there is trying to kill me. Who *is* she, anyway?" She pointed accusingly at

Sharpay.

The director put his hands on his hips. "Excellent question," he remarked, giving Sharpay a cold stare.

"I can explain!" Sharpay cried. "My name is Sharpay Evans. I'm an actress, and all I want is a chance to show you that I..."

The director didn't wait to hear anymore. He lifted his bullhorn to his lips. "Security!" he bellowed.

Meanwhile, Gabriella couldn't believe how much fun she was having learning how to surf! She and her friends had been practising all day, except for a break for a relaxed lunchtime picnic that Mrs Evans had catered for them right on the beach.

Now they were all back in the water. Gabriella had just caught a decent-size wave, and after paddling along with it for a moment, she smoothly brought her feet under her and stood up. She wobbled for a moment but quickly regained her balance. Gabriella then bent her knees and held her arms out to steady herself. Her heart pounded as she rode the wave toward shore. It was an awesome feeling – almost as exciting as stepping onstage to sing in the school musical!

"Way to go!" Trish whooped. She ran through the shallow water to meet Gabriella as she glided in. "That was your best ride yet. You're totally a natural at this!"

"Thanks!" Gabriella beamed as she hopped off her board. "But you deserve a lot of the credit. You're a great teacher."

Trish raised her hand for a high five. "We make an awesome team," she agreed.

Gabriella grinned and slapped her hand. As she turned to check the ankle leash on her surfboard, she noticed Troy staring at her with an anxious crease in his forehead.

She sighed, a flash of irritation dampening her enjoyment for a second. He'd been looking at her like that all day.

Sharpay and Ryan trudged along a dingy city

street. The sweltering California sunshine beat down on them, reflecting up off the sidewalk so that it felt as if they were walking in a giant concrete oven. The street was jammed with heavy traffic, choking them with exhaust fumes and making them jump every time one of the cars blew its horn.

Ryan clicked his mobile phone shut. "Dad's limo driver can't come pick us up," he reported.

"Give me that." Sharpay snatched the phone. Flipping it open, she dialled information. "I'm calling a cab," she told her brother. "It's after five o'clock. There's no point in trying another studio now. We might as well go back to the beach house."

She was in a bad mood. A *very* bad mood. That movie-musical director had kicked them off the lot. No one had seemed to care that they were the children of Vance Evans, the successful film producer.

They headed to the nearest corner to wait for their taxi. While they were standing there, a mother and her young daughter crossed the street toward them. The little girl was clutching a small teddy bear with a big pink bow around its neck. The girl's big blue eyes widened, and she pointed at Sharpay.

"Mummy, is that a movie star?" she asked excitedly.

"Shhh," the mother whispered. "It's not polite to point."

Sharpay's mood lightened a bit. "Well, hello there," she cooed at the little girl. "Aren't you adorable? Is that your teddy?"

"Uh-huh. Her name is Pumpkin." The little girl blinked up at Sharpay. "You're pretty. What movies are you in?"

"Aren't you sweet!" Sharpay patted her on the head. "I'm not in any movies quite yet," she added. "But you'll start seeing me up on the silver screen soon. Very, very soon."

"Come along, Lucy." The mother tugged on her daughter's hand, shooting Sharpay a vaguely suspicious look. "We're going to be late to meet your daddy at the hotel."

"Wait." Sharpay grabbed the girl's bear. "Do

you have a pen? I'll sign Pumpkin for you, all right? That way when I win my first Academy Award, you'll be able to tell all of your friends that you have my autograph."

Ryan took a pen out of his messenger bag and handed it to Sharpay. She took it and signed the bear's stomach with a flourish. She noticed that the girl's mother had pulled her daughter a little closer, keeping a tight grip on her hand. But Sharpay didn't care. She was sure the woman would be bragging to all her friends about this encounter once Sharpay hit it big.

"There you go, sweetheart." Sharpay handed the bear back to its owner. "Remember to follow your dreams, okay?"

The second the bear was back in little Lucy's arms, the mother bustled her daughter off down the street. But Lucy glanced over her shoulder and waved at Sharpay. Sharpay smiled and waved back.

She tossed the pen back to Ryan. "I think I've realized what we did wrong today," she told him, her enthusiasm coming back after the encounter with her young fan. "In Hollywood, it's not about how talented you are or what you know; it's all about *who* you know. I'll just have to be better organized tomorrow, that's all. I need to make Daddy help me out more, work his contacts, that sort of thing. After all, we've only got three more days here to make me a star, and I don't want to waste a second of them!"

CHAPTER SEVEN

"Look at that." Jason sighed happily and gazed out across the deck at the morning sun gleaming off the ocean. "Another perfect California morning."

"Of course!" Taylor exclaimed, looking up from her cereal. "Isn't that pretty much guaranteed in the state constitution? At least three hundred sixty-four gorgeous, sunny days per year?"

Troy chuckled along with the others. They were lingering over breakfast, enjoying the nice weather and the feeling of being on vacation.

The food was delicious, the company was great, and Troy couldn't think of anywhere he'd rather be at the moment. He smiled across the table at Gabriella, who looked radiant in a sky blue tank top and matching headband. He reached out to help himself to another slice of fresh pineapple.

"Leave some for the rest of us, dude!" Chad joked.

Troy grinned. "Hey, what can I say? All that surfing yesterday worked up an appetite!"

Just then, Sharpay strode onto the deck. Ryan, looking a little weary, followed behind her. While everyone else was casually dressed in shorts and T-shirts, Sharpay was wearing silver capri trousers, high heels and a sparkly pink halter top. Her hair and make-up were flawless, as always.

"Looking good, Sharpay," Zeke commented. "Did you two finish your business stuff yesterday? Because we're thinking of heading over to Venice Beach this morning, then meeting Banzai and the others for more surfing after lunch. What do you say?"

"No time for that sort of frivolous tourism today, I'm afraid," Sharpay replied haughtily. She grabbed a piece of whole-wheat toast off the table. "I have a full day of appointments with agents and casting directors. I'm going to have to hurry as it is just to squeeze in all the people who want to meet with me."

"Oh." Zeke looked disappointed. "Well, that sounds fun, too."

"Oh, I'm sure it will be *very* rewarding. Toodles!" Sharpay waggled her fingers at the group and hurried off. Ryan shrugged at Zeke, snatched a banana out of the fruit bowl and ran after her.

"Wow, it seems as if Sharpay and Ryan aren't letting themselves have any fun at all on this trip," Gabriella said.

Chad nodded. "I hear you," he agreed. "It sure doesn't seem like they're tuned in to the whole holiday vibe."

"Yeah." Troy stared off in the direction Sharpay and her brother had gone. "I don't get it. Why would they want to waste the few days we have here in L.A., rushing around when they could be enjoying themselves?"

Sharpay tapped her foot impatiently. She checked her watch for about the fifth time in the past minute. She'd been waiting more than half an hour in the cramped waiting room of a top Hollywood agent's office. She glared at the agent's assistant, who had been studiously ignoring them since telling them to have a seat.

This was her third appointment of the day, and Sharpay couldn't help feeling a bit discouraged by her lack of progress. But she comforted herself with the thought that everything would be very different soon. When she was a big star, other people would be waiting around for *her*!

"Maybe we should call it a day," Ryan suggested hopefully.

Sharpay shot him an annoyed look. "Way to be supportive, brother dear," she said sarcastically.

Ryan sat up straight in his chair. "I just don't see the point," he argued. "This guy, if he ever lets us in, is probably just going to say the same thing as the last two – don't call us, we'll call – "

Before Ryan could finish, the phone on the assistant's desk buzzed loudly. "Quiet!" Sharpay hissed. "This could be it."

The assistant picked up the phone, listened for a moment, and hung up. She glanced at Sharpay, clearly disinterested. "Mr Jones will see you now, Miss Stevens," she reported.

"It's *Evans*. And it's about time!" Sharpay jumped to her feet, adjusted her halter top, and quickly checked her hair and teeth in the mirror on the wall of the waiting room. She strode over to the office door and let herself and Ryan in.

A short, stout man was sitting behind an enormous mahogany desk covered with papers. A notice board on the wall behind him was crammed with head shots of actors. Sharpay's eyes widened slightly as she recognized several well-known faces among them. *Now* she was getting somewhere. This guy was clearly big-time! That was perfect, because she was ready to wow him – *big-time*.

"Good morning, Mr Jones," she began in her

most chipper voice. "My name is Sharpay Evans, and I'm just the kind of fresh new talent you've been looking – "

"I don't have much time," the agent interrupted brusquely. "Got a conference call with De Niro in five. Can the speech and get on with it."

"Oh. Um, okay." Sharpay blinked. "Well, would you like to see a dramatic monologue? It really shows off my – "

At that moment, the phone on the desk rang. "Jones here," the agent barked into the receiver, cutting Sharpay off again. "Oh! Glad you called. I've been waiting to hear from you."

Sharpay couldn't help feeling a flash of irritation. Did he have to take a phone call in the middle of their meeting? Wasn't that what his assistant was for? Still, she supposed it was understandable. The person on the other end of the line was probably one of his glittering roster of superstar clients. Perhaps it was some world-famous actress, calling in from her movie set somewhere halfway around the globe....

"Great. I'm glad the stain came out," the

agent was saying, and something resembling a smile lightened his intense expression for a moment. "I'll have my assistant pick up the suits and drop off those shirts. Just don't forget to make a note about the garment bags."

Sharpay's heart sank as she realized the truth. He wasn't talking to some Academy Award-winning client. He had taken a call from his *dry cleaner*! Talk about humiliation...

But she wasn't going to let the man's rudeness stop her from winning him over. Realizing that it might not be the best time for her dramatic monologue, she decided to skip ahead to her song-and-dance number. That was sure to grab his attention.

When Mr Jones hung up the phone, Sharpay poked Ryan in the shoulder. "From the top!" she cried.

Ryan looked startled. But he caught on quickly when Sharpay burst into song. She put everything she had into the performance, each note and every dance step bursting with energy.

But they hadn't even finished the first verse

when the agent stood up abruptly. "Gotta go," he said with a glance at his watch. "We'll be in touch if we're interested."

Without waiting for a response, he strode out of the room. Sharpay stared after him, a bit stunned by the curt dismissal.

"See what I mean?" Ryan asked with a sigh. "This is a waste of time. Face it, Sharpay. The only reason these people agreed to see you at all is because Dad twisted their arms."

"Maybe so. But all I need is *one* of those people to pay attention and recognize my huge potential, and it'll all be worth it." Sharpay glanced up at the famous faces on the agent's bulletin board. Seeing them renewed her determination. "Now, come on — we need to hurry if we want to make it to that casting call across town."

"*You* need to hurry." Ryan frowned. "I've had enough. I'm going back to the beach house."

Sharpay glared at him. "You *can't* be serious!"

"You're right," he said. "I can't be serious about this anymore. I'd much rather be *un*serious and finally have some fun on this trip with our friends." Ryan turned on one heel and stomped away.

"Fine! I can do this without you!" Sharpay shouted after him as he left the office. "And I'll be sure *not* to thank you in my acceptance speech when I win my first Academy Award!"

CHAPTER EIGHT

"**R**yan! Over here!" Kelsi waved as she spotted Ryan jogging down the beach toward the group.

"When did you get back?" Taylor asked.

"Where's Sharpay?" Zeke asked brightly.

"Just now, and I have no idea." Ryan smiled tentatively. "Did I miss all the surfing?"

"No way!" Chad exclaimed.

"We just got out here ourselves," Gabriella said. "Come over and meet – "

"Our professors of wave-ology," Chad finished as Gabriella gave him a wide smile.

The group led Ryan over to meet the surfers. After introductions had been made, everyone got down to business. Before long, Ryan had caught on to the basics.

"Hey, this is kind of fun!" he exclaimed, as Louie showed him how to stand up on the board while it was safely planted on dry sand. "It's sort of like dancing!"

Louie chuckled. "That's right, dude," he agreed. "You're dancing with the ocean."

"Dancing with the ocean. I like that." Ryan smiled.

"Hey, Louie!" Gabriella ran up, breathless and drenched from her last wave. "You promised to teach me some new moves today, remember? How about it?" Suddenly noticing Ryan, she smiled apologetically. "Oh! Sorry. Are you still busy with Ryan's lesson?"

"No, it's okay. You can go ahead." Ryan bent his knees, practising the moves Louie had just showed him. "I'll just practise on my own for a while."

"Cool. Come on." Louie grinned at Gabriella and tilted his head toward the ocean.

As the two of them ran off into the surf, Ryan hopped off his board and wandered over to where Troy and Chad were standing nearby.

"This is great," Ryan said. "I wish I'd come with you to Venice Beach this morning, too. Did you guys have fun?"

"Uh-huh." Troy barely heard him. He was concentrating on Gabriella as she paddled out into the surf with Louie.

"Don't even try to have a conversation with him," Chad advised, rolling his eyes. "He's afraid Gabriella might chip a nail or something."

Jason and Martha overheard what they were talking about as they passed by.

"Actually, Gabriella's doing terrific," Martha said.

Jason agreed. "You need to chill, Troy...."

"Are you guys talking about Gabriella?" Kelsi hurried over, too. "Can you believe how fast she's learning all those tricky moves? She's amazing."

"See?" Chad grinned and slapped Troy on the back. "Guess you didn't have to worry that Gabriella wouldn't be able to handle surfing."

"Huh?" Troy blinked at him. "What do you mean?"

"Just look at her, man." Jason gestured toward the water.

Troy turned just in time to see Gabriella catch a wave. She paddled to get in position, then popped up on her board, balancing effortlessly. Louie and the other two champion surfers whooped and cheered as she glided in to shore with a big smile on her face.

"Wow," Troy said. "She *is* getting good, isn't she?"

He couldn't help being a little surprised. Somehow he'd been so busy worrying abut her that he hadn't even noticed how good she was.

"Okay, this is *so* not what I was expecting," Sharpay muttered, folding her arms across her chest and frowning. She was standing in a long line of aspiring young actresses outside a casting office. When her father's secretary had told her when and where to show up to try out for an upcoming movie, Sharpay had been expecting a private audition. Unfortunately, it had turned out to be an open casting call.

The line edged forward slightly. This is even worse than those ridiculous open auditions for the musicals back home! Sharpay thought. There have to be a million people here trying out for, um...

Realizing she still didn't have all the information she needed, Sharpay turned to a girl with spiky black hair and a nose ring who was behind her in line. "Hey," she said. "What role is this tryout for, anyway?"

The girl looked at her strangely. "Why are you here if you don't even know *that*?"

"If you must know, I have a *lot* of meetings and auditions today," Sharpay said frostily. "I just, um, forgot which one this is."

The girl shrugged. "It's a horror movie about zombies."

"Oh." Sharpay wasn't sure she liked the sound of that. When she imagined her big break, it wasn't in some low-budget horror film. But she supposed it didn't matter. In fact, it might make a cute anecdote to tell during interviews later in her career. "Is it for the lead?" she asked hopefully.

The girl laughed. She peered at Sharpay through her charcoal-lined eyes. Sharpay stared blankly back at her.

"Oh, you're serious?" the girl asked. "Uh, no. This open call is for 'Screaming Girl number three.'"

Sharpay *definitely* didn't like the sound of that. *Screaming Girl number three*? That had to be the movie equivalent of being stuck in the last row of the chorus in a stage musical! Still, she'd stood here this long – she supposed she might as well go through with the audition. Maybe if she impressed the casting director, he or she would find a better part for her. Maybe they'd even decide to cast her in an entirely different movie – say, one where she could co-star with some dreamy hunk and become the toast of Hollywood virtually overnight....

Sharpay was still daydreaming about that when her turn finally came. "Wish me luck!" she yelled to the girl she had been talking to, and then she hurried into the office.

Three people were sitting at a table inside. The

red-haired woman in the middle seemed to be in charge. "Name?" she asked.

"Sharpay Evans!" Sharpay exclaimed eagerly. "I've been acting, singing, and dancing my whole life and I –"

"That's fine," the red-haired woman broke in. "I'm the casting director and here's what I need you to do. Run a few steps while looking over your shoulder. It's as if you're being chased by a hideous zombie. After that, scream and pretend to faint. Got it?"

"Got it," Sharpay repeated. She took a deep breath and rolled her head from side to side. Next she did her favourite warm-up exercise, which involved blowing out her breath in a sort of highpitched descending scale while wriggling her fingers in front of her. Finally she closed her eyes, envisioning what it would be like to be chased by the undead....

"Any day now," the casting director interrupted impatiently.

Sharpay opened her eyes. All three of the people at the table were staring at her.

"Okay, I'm ready," she announced.

She cleared her throat. Backing up against one wall of the office, she ran a few steps across the room. She glanced back over her shoulder and widened her eyes in mock terror.

"Oh, my stars!" she exclaimed in a British accent. "I never believed in zombies, but they're real! *They're real!*"

"Hold it!" The casting director held up one hand. "What was that?"

Sharpay shrugged. "I was just doing what you said. Acting as if I were running away from a horrible zombie."

"This is a *nonspeaking* role," the woman said. "And the movie is set in Cleveland, not London."

"But I thought you would want to see that I can act..." Sharpay replied, "...just to be sure I can handle anything the part might require."

"We're not casting *Hamlet* here," one of the men at the table said sarcastically. "We just need a pretty girl who can scream."

The other man glanced at his watch. "Right. And there are plenty of girls outside waiting their turn."

"Sorry." Sharpay couldn't understand why they didn't appreciate the depth she'd brought to the audition. But she wasn't going to argue. At least not until *after* they hired her and realized she knew what she was talking about. "Can I try it one more time – please?"

The red-haired woman leaned back and crossed her arms. "Fine. But let's make sure we hear some screaming this time."

Once again, Sharpay took a deep breath and backed up against the wall. Since she wasn't supposed to speak, she figured she would have to show the breadth of her talent in some other way. So she added a touch from her ballet training and leaped several steps across the floor.

With that, she glanced over her shoulder and screamed. But it was no ordinary scream. It began sort of low, climbed up an octave, and came back down again, ending with a little vibrato. At the same time, she pretended to weaken. Just as she almost fell, she caught herself. She staggered forward a step or two, then feigned almost passing out in fear before jerking back up again.

"Thank you," the casting director cut her off just as she was preparing to finally crumple dramatically to the floor. "I think we've seen enough."

"Wait!" Sharpay straightened up, feeling panicked. "If you didn't like that, I can give you something else. Maybe if I knew a little more about what my motivation is supposed to be in this scene..."

The casting director just shuffled the papers in front of her and glanced over at the assistant standing by the door. "Next!"

CHAPTER NINE

Troy kicked strongly against the pull of the surf. He aimed for the spot where he and the others had been picking up waves all day. Out of the corner of his eye, he saw Gabriella heading over to him.

"This is amazing, isn't it?" she called over with a smile.

"Uh-huh." He winced as a wave smacked the front of her surfboard, splashing foam into her face. But she just laughed and shook her head to clear it from her eyes.

There was no more time to watch her. A wave was coming, and Troy knew he had to time things right if he wanted to catch it. He could only hope that his friends were right, and Gabriella could handle herself out here.

They both went for it at the same time, just a few yards apart. Gabriella got the wave at exactly the right moment, popping up onto her board and skillfully riding in to the beach.

Troy wasn't so lucky. He thought he'd timed it right. But just as he planted his feet on the board and let go with his hands, the wave seemed to shift beneath him. He ended up wiping out and being tossed toward the shore.

"Troy! Are you okay?" Troy came up sputtering in the shallow surf, with water in his eyes and sand in his shorts. He sat up and pushed the wet hair out of his face as Gabriella hurried toward him, looking concerned.

"I'm fine," he said breathlessly. "But I think I'm finally starting to see what the other guys were talking about."

"Huh?" She looked confused.

"Come on," he said. "Can we talk for a minute?"

They walked back to their blankets, sat down on their surfboards, and faced each other.

"Listen." Troy leaned forward. "I'm sorry, Gabriella."

"For what?" She peered at him curiously. "Did you hit your head on your surfboard when you fell?"

"No, but I think I might've just knocked some sense into myself." He smiled ruefully. "All this time I've been watching you out there, worried that you were going to hurt yourself. I just immediately assumed you couldn't handle surfing as well as I could." He took Gabriella's hand. "But if I'd actually let myself pay attention for a moment, I would have realized a lot sooner that you're doing totally fine. You're doing fantastic, actually! I'm just sorry it took me this long."

"Oh!" She looked surprised. Then she smiled back. "I appreciate that you care about me that much, Troy. I like that you want to come to my rescue, but I can stick up for myself and brave the waves on my own sometimes. You know?"

"I do," replied Troy, nodding. "And I know there will probably be times when I still worry about you, but that doesn't mean I don't believe in you. I'll never make that mistake again."

Gabriella smiled. "Thank you," she said. "So ...does this mean you think I can be athletic – even if I'm *not* a superstar basketball player?" she teased.

"Absolutely. Already, you're way better than me at surfing." Troy dropped her hand and stood up. "But not quite athletic enough to beat me back to the house for a glass of lemonade!"

"Oh, yeah? We'll see about that!" Laughing, she sprang up and dashed off across the sand.

That night, the whole gang had a bonfire and barbecue on the beach. The three surfers came, and even Sharpay showed up eventually, after her long day of appointments and auditions.

Ryan felt kind of guilty when he saw his sister moping. He wondered if he should have stuck it out and helped Sharpay live her dream. But he tried not to think about that as he chatted with Banzai, Trish, Martha, and Zeke.

"This is fun," Banzai said. "We should do it again tomorrow night."

"We can't." Zeke tossed the foam football he was holding from one hand to the other. "Tomorrow is that premiere we told you about."

"The one for the movie Ryan's dad pro-duced," Martha explained.

"That's right," said Ryan, suddenly getting an idea. "Hey!" he blurted out. "Why don't you guys come along?"

"For real?" Trish looked excited. "That would be amazing, but are you sure your dad won't mind?"

"No way! He'll love it. I'll go tell him right now and make sure he reserves enough seats." Ryan took off for the house at top speed.

Sharpay looked up to see her brother running off. She didn't know what that was about, and she didn't care. Her day had been exhausting and more than a little frustrating. So far, her triumphant arrival in Hollywood wasn't anything like what she'd expected. Worse yet, she wasn't sure what to do about it.

"Hi, Sharpay!" Zeke greeted her eagerly as the two surfers and Martha drifted off to talk to Taylor and Chad. "How was your day?"

"Don't ask." She grimaced.

Zeke shrugged. "Okay. But you're at the beach now, so that means you have to start having fun."

"Says who?"

"Says me. And if you don't, this is what happens." Zeke bounced his foam football off her head.

"Hey!" Sharpay grabbed the ball. "Stop that."

"Give me the ball back!" Zeke exclaimed, holding out his hands.

Sharpay grinned. "No way. Hey Kelsi – catch! And don't let Zeke get it!" She flung the ball at Kelsi, who was walking by.

Kelsi caught the ball, looking startled. As Zeke barrelled toward her, arms outstretched, she let out a squeak and quickly tossed it back to Sharpay.

"That's it!" Sharpay was actually laughing by now. "This thing's going in the ocean. So say good-bye, Zeke!" She took off at full speed for the water's edge, giggling and glancing back over her shoulder as Zeke chased her.

The gang spent the entire next day at the beach surfing and hanging out. Well, except for Sharpay. She headed to the local spa right after breakfast. There was a lot to do to prepare for that night's premiere. She needed to get a manicure and a pedicure, her hair highlighted, a massage, an avocado facial, and a soothing seaweed body wrap.

As late afternoon approached, it was time to head to the theatre. Everyone crowded into the stretch limo Mr Evans had hired. The three young surfers came, too, looking totally different in their formal attire, but acting just as cool and laid back as always.

Taylor wriggled in her seat in the limo. "My feet hurt," she complained. "I don't know why I couldn't wear normal shoes. It's not like anyone's going to be looking at me with all those movie stars around."

"Since we're so close to the beach, maybe we can all go barefoot?" Martha suggested.

Sharpay shot her a horrified look. "Don't you dare!" she ordered. "And don't be so sure nobody will be looking at you....You're with me. I mean, us. Daddy *is* one of the primary producers, you know."

Just then the limo pulled in front of the theatre.

"Wow!" Troy exclaimed. "Check it out!"

Gabriella stared out the window, wide-eyed. "There are tons of people outside!" she cried.

"And photographers," Chad added, crowding in beside her for a look.

"It's just like on TV!" Kelsi and Ryan exclaimed at the same time and smiled.

Flashbulbs popped around them as the limo door opened and they climbed out. "This way!" Sharpay called, herding them toward the red carpet. "Keep moving. Nobody cares about any of you."

Jason had a puzzled look on his face. "That's not what she said a minute ago," he whispered to Taylor and Kelsi.

When the others had gone on ahead, Sharpay hung back. She'd chosen her dress carefully so as to be as photogenic as possible when she walked down the red carpet. She realized that tonight could be her last chance to make a good impression on the Hollywood elite, and she didn't want to miss her opportunity. When she reached the biggest cluster of photographers, she paused and struck a pose. To her dismay, though, none of them took her picture. In fact, they were all craning their necks to look past her.

"It's them!" one of them cried hoarsely. "Here they come!"

"Zarina! Trent! Over here!" several of the photographers called out as a willowy young woman, who was holding the hand of a good-looking actor, headed toward Sharpay.

"Move it," one photographer added with a glance at Sharpay.

"Well!" she exclaimed, stalking off after her friends. Just see if she ever gave any of *those* photographers the time of day once she was famous!

Inside the theatre was another crush of people. Sharpay began to circulate, keeping an eye out for anyone important. If she could make some decent contacts here, maybe this trip wouldn't turn out to be a total waste after all....

"Well, hello there, miss," someone said. "I haven't seen you at one of these events before. Are you in this film?"

Sharpay turned to see a short, balding man in a baggy suit peering up at her through horn-rimmed glasses.

"Excuse me," she said frostily. "Do I know you?"

The man shrugged. "Not yet," he replied mildly. "But I – "

"Oh, my gosh!" Sharpay gasped, spotting a very tall man entering the room. "Isn't that Sky-High Marco over there?"

She rushed off without a backward glance. The basketball-star-turned-actor was surrounded by admirers, but she pushed through them quickly.

"Mr Sky-High!" she cried. "It's so nice to meet you! I'm Sharpay Evans, and I'm a big fan."

The star smiled distantly down at her. "Thanks," he said. "Excuse me."

He walked off, leaving Sharpay feeling snubbed and irritated. "Fine," she muttered. "Your career is a joke anyway. Being able to slam-dunk a basketball has *nothing* to do with a slam dunk at the box office."

She scanned the room. The man who had approached her earlier was still standing nearby, and he lifted his glass in a friendly way when she glanced at him. She sighed. He certainly didn't look like an important agent. After all, he wasn't surrounded by any celebrity clients. She turned away in search of someone worth talking to.

"This is pretty unreal, isn't it?" Troy sipped his club soda, looking around the spacious theatre lobby, which was getting more crowded every minute. It was a little intimidating to be among so many famous faces. But it was fun, too.

Gabriella, Trish, and Louie nodded. They had lost track of the rest of their group for the moment, although every so often the sound of Sharpay's distinctive laugh rose above the noise of the crowd.

"I guess you guys do this sort of thing all the time back home, huh?" Louie joked as the four of them watched the star of a hit sitcom walk past them.

Troy and Gabriella laughed and traded a glance. "Not exactly," Gabriella replied. "It's more about the Scholastic Decathlon competitions and basketball tournaments for us, right, Troy?"

"Right," he agreed. "Plus a little singing now and then. But *not* the kind of singing *she* does." His eyes widened as an international pop star shimmied across the room in a silver-beaded dress.

Trish took a sip of her cranberry juice. "Yeah, same for us," she said. "I mean, not the singing part. But we don't usually hang out with this kind of crowd. We're so stoked that Ryan invited us!"

Suddenly, a nondescript man with horn-rimmed glasses shambled up to them. He looked rather out of place among all the glittering stars. He gave the group a friendly smile.

"Pardon me," he said modestly. "I don't mean to interrupt. But aren't you Louie Kelly, Trish Waverly, and Bob 'Banzai' Santos, the famous surfers?"

Louie laughed. "This is the *last* place I expected to get recognized, dude," he said. "But totally – that's us."

"Wonderful!" The man looked pleased. "I'd love to talk to you for a moment. My name is – "

"Guys!" Zeke rushed up with what appeared to be strawberry frosting on his upper lip. "You have *got* to see the buffet. Croissants, cannolis, cream puffs, sponge cake, tiramisu, éclairs, baklava – I've never seen so many amazing desserts all in one place before!" Finally, he breathed. "And it's all *free*!"

He dragged a laughing Troy and Gabriella off with him, leaving the surfers to chat with the mystery man.

CHAPTER TEN

Sharpay squeezed herself into the crowd surrounding rap star Flashy J. He had just arrived at the premiere, complete with a large entourage and his trademark fluffy fake-fur coat. He was being interviewed by a reporter from *Tinseltown Today*.

"What are you working on these days, Flashy?" the perky blond reporter asked, holding a microphone in front of him.

"Well," Flashy J replied, "my new album drops – " He cut himself off as Sharpay worked her way to a spot right behind the reporter. "Hey there, gorgeous," he said to her, his smile revealing several platinum-capped teeth.

Sharpay smiled back. At last, someone important had noticed her. It was about time!

The star shrugged off his fur coat. "Here you go, darling," he said, tossing it to Sharpay. "Make sure you put it on a wide wooden hanger, all right?"

Sharpay was so stunned that she couldn't react for a moment. Before she knew it, she'd been shuffled back into the crowd, still clutching the enormous wad of fake fur. She stared down at it as the truth slowly dawned on her. Flashy J hadn't recognized her beauty and talent. He had mistaken her for the *coat-check girl*!

She stomped over to the coat-check area and tossed the fake fur onto the counter. "Put it on a wire hanger," she ordered the girl behind the counter. "A rusty one, if you have it!" Without waiting for a response, she stomped away.

It was almost time for the movie to begin, and the crowd was starting to file into the theatre.

Sharpay spotted her parents and Ryan and hurried to join them.

"There you are, princess," her father greeted her. "Come on, let's get to our seats. They're right up front."

Sharpay smiled to herself. Her family's seats were indeed among the best in the house. But she was still distracted as the lights went down and the film started to roll. She sat there, tapping her foot for a few minutes and staring blankly at the screen. Finally, she couldn't take it anymore. It was fine for all these other people to sit around staring slack-jawed at the movie screen. But she had more important things to do.

"Excuse me," she whispered to her family. "I'll be right back."

She climbed out over the rest of the row, barely noticing the dismayed grunt when she stepped on someone's foot. Soon she was out in the quiet lobby. She wasn't quite sure what to do next, but she figured she had a much better chance of running into someone important out here than she did sitting in her seat in the dark.

When a few minutes passed and nobody came out, she got impatient. She wandered into the ladies' room, hoping that some female star might be touching up her make-up. But the only person in there was a washroom attendant who stared at Sharpay suspiciously anytime she got too close to the tip jar.

Finally, Sharpay gave up and went back into the darkened theatre. "Where were you?" Ryan whispered as she sat down.

"Just getting some fresh air," she whispered back. "What did I miss?"

"A lot!" Ryan whispered, sounding excited. "See, there's this guy, and he gets kicked out of his college...."

"Never mind." Sharpay waved her hand. "I'll catch up."

But once again, she couldn't focus on the movie. Only ten or fifteen minutes had passed when she got up again.

Back in the lobby, she made a beeline for the restroom. She'd just had a brilliant idea.

Everyone had taken full advantage of the free drinks and food at the buffet before the screening. Surely at least one of the women would need to visit the facilities at some point. Maybe it would be somebody famous! And Sharpay planned to be there when it happened.

"What are you doing, miss?" the bathroom attendant demanded as Sharpay ducked into one stall after the other, removing all the toilet paper. "You can't do that!"

"My father paid for this toilet paper," Sharpay snapped. "I can do whatever I want with it."

She crammed the last roll into the cabinet under the sink and smiled. Now they'll *have* to talk to me, she thought with satisfaction. If only to ask for help. That's all the opening I need....

"Move, girlie." The washroom attendant gave Sharpay a shove. "This place is *my* gig. Go find your own." She grabbed the toilet paper and started redistributing it to its proper places.

"Hey!" Sharpay protested.

The woman turned and glared at her. "And

keep your paws off my tips if you know what's good for you!"

Sharpay was still slumped in the lobby trying to think of another plan when the theatre doors burst open and people began pouring out. A few minutes later, she spotted her family and friends near the front of the crowd. They were all smiling and chattering eagerly about the film.

"Hey, what happened to you?" Ryan asked when he spotted Sharpay. "You missed the whole thing!"

Sharpay let out a sigh. "I guess I did."

Sharpay woke up on Saturday morning feeling depressed. She threw on the first thing she found in her suitcase – just a boring old rhinestone-studded tank top and black satin shorts – and dragged herself downstairs. The others had already eaten breakfast and gone outside for one last day on the beach. Sharpay just sat there alone at the table, picking at her blueberry muffin.

Her father wandered in after a while and headed for the coffeepot. "There you are, sleepy-head," he greeted her cheerfully. "What's on the agenda for today? Want me to call more of my contacts so you can squeeze in a few more auditions?"

"No, thanks, Daddy," she said flatly. What was the point? She felt totally defeated.

Her father gave her a sympathetic look and walked out of the room. Just then, Ryan hurried in from outside. "Hey, you're awake," he said when he saw Sharpay.

"Yeah," she muttered. "But I'm not that particularly happy about it."

He smiled faintly. "So are you coming to the beach today? It'll be fun."

"Why not?" Sharpay shrugged. "It's not like I have anything better to do."

They found the other Wildcats gathered in their usual surfing spot, though their new surfer friends weren't with them. "Still no sign of those three, huh?" Ryan asked.

Zeke shook his head. "Maybe they're sleeping

in. We *were* out pretty late last night at that premiere." His eyes brightened as he saw Sharpay. "Hey, Sharpay," he said. "You came! Want me to teach you some surfing moves?"

She sighed deeply, too weary to argue. "I suppose."

They all hung out for a while, goofing off and having fun. Zeke's sunny mood started to rub off on Sharpay, and gradually her spirits lifted a little. It really *was* kind of fun to be at the beach with her friends. And besides, even movie stars had to take a break now and then to relax and recharge. At least now she would have one day of that. Okay, so it wasn't quite as much fun as if she'd landed a starring role in some blockbuster film. But she supposed she would have to take what she could get.

A few minutes later, Troy's mobile phone rang. He answered and listened for a second. "It's Trish," he called to the others. "She wants us to meet her and the guys at some hot surfing spot a little farther down the beach. Says it's where the waves are happening today."

"So what are we waiting for?" Chad grabbed his board. "Let's go!"

When they arrived at the designated spot, the Wildcats were surprised to find a film crew setting up on the beach. "Huh?" Jason scratched his head and stared.

Trish, Louie and Banzai spotted them and ran over. "Surprise!" Trish cried. "We're going to be on TV!"

"You are?" Taylor blinked.

Louie laughed. "Not just us," he corrected. "You guys, too. We're all going to be in an episode of *Malibu Prep!*"

After that, everyone started talking over each other. It was a few minutes before they all calmed down enough to get the whole story. It turned out that the man with the horn-rimmed glasses from the night before was a very successful TV director. He was planning to shoot a beach scene today for the popular teen drama. When he'd recognized the teen surfers at the premiere, he'd invited them to appear in the scene as stunt doubles and also in cameo roles as themselves.

But that wasn't all. It turned out that he also needed some teenage extras for the scene. And luckily, the young surfers knew some available teens who fit the bill!

"So what do you say?" Banzai asked with a grin. "You dudes ready to make your TV debut?"

Chad stroked his chin with mock doubt. "Well, I don't know," he said. "I should check with my agent...."

"Don't listen to him!" Sharpay shoved her way to the front. "We'll do it!"

Before long, all the Wildcats were rushing around between the costume truck and the hair and make-up tents, preparing for their roles as extras. Sharpay was living it up, enjoying every second.

"You there!" she called, snapping her fingers at a production assistant. "I asked for a bottle of water ten minutes ago. So where is it?"

Chad rolled his eyes. "Chill, Sharpay," he said. "You'd think you were the star of the show instead of an extra like the rest of us."

Sharpay shrugged. "Everyone has to start

somewhere. This might be *your* only chance to appear on TV, but it's only the first step in *my* fabulous career." She glanced around impatiently. "Now, where's that make-up girl?"

Zeke laughed. "Leave her alone, man," he said, clapping Chad on the back. "She's just being Sharpay."

Ryan chuckled along with the others. He was sure that with her determination, his sister would make all her dreams come true. He just hoped Sharpay didn't forget to take time to have fun along the way!

Something new is on the way!
Look for the next book in the Disney High
School Musical: Stories from East High series...

BONJOUR, WILDCATS!

By N.B. Grace
Based on the Disney Channel Original Movie
"High School Musical," Written by Peter Barsocchini
Based on "High School Musical 2," Written by Peter Barsocchini
Based on Characters Created by Peter Barsocchini

Good morning! Welcome to another *wonderful* Monday!" Ms Darbus called out over the chatter in her homeroom class. The noise increased as everyone tried to say one more thing to a friend before it was time to be quiet and listen to the morning announcements.

Ms Darbus clapped her hands for silence. "Settle down, everyone." There were a few scattered groans, and then the noise finally subsided, with only a few whispers scattered around the room. "Thank you," Ms Darbus said. She added dryly, "I know Mondays are *terribly* exciting, but we must control our extreme glee at being back at school after what was undoubtedly a long, boring, practically endless weekend."

"Yeah, Saturdays just seem to go on *forever*," Chad Danforth joked. "I mean, there's never anything to do! Well, except catch a movie."

"Or shoot some hoops," his friend, Troy Bolton, chimed in.

"Or play video games," Jason Cross added.

"Or maybe go for a bike ride," Zeke Baylor finished up.

But Chad shook his head, pretending to look pained at all these suggestions. "No, guys, face it, weekends are endless wastes of time, just waiting to be filled with pointless activity." He folded his hands on his desk and looked earnestly at their homeroom teacher. "You're so right, Ms Darbus. I can hardly wait to get to calculus class."

Across the aisle, Taylor McKessie rolled her eyes. Chad grinned at her and said, "I know, I know, you actually *are* looking forward to calculus."

"We're going to learn about the Riemann integral today, so, yes, Chad, I am looking forward to it," Taylor replied with a huff.

"You are so lucky to have me around to keep you from turning into a total grind," Chad said jokingly.

Gabriella Montez glanced over at Troy and caught his eye. They both grinned. It was always fun to see Chad tease Taylor and then watch Taylor pretend she didn't like it.

"Well, it *is* fun to come to school when you can see all your friends," Gabriella said under her breath so that only Troy would hear it. "Especially since this is sometimes the only place where that happens!"

He gave her an understanding wink. Troy and Gabriella usually hung out quite a bit in their free time, but the last two weekends had been so packed with basketball games, family gatherings and homework that they had only managed a couple of hurried phone conversations. "At least nothing's going on this weekend," he whispered back, just as the late bell rang.

Ms Darbus rapped on her desk with her ruler. "Actually, this Monday is a little more exciting than most," she said to the class, "because we have a surprise in store –"

Before she could finish, Sharpay Evans and her brother, Ryan, bounded breathlessly into the room. Sharpay was wearing a pink skirt covered with blue flowers, a short white jacket over a turquoise T-shirt, and a long purple scarf. Ryan's outfit was more subdued in comparison, but he had decided that a brown tweed fedora was a good match for tan pants and a pink and white striped shirt. They both looked ultra-fashionable, as usual.

Gabriella thought that if she had been late, she would have slunk into her seat, blushing with embarrassment. But Sharpay and Ryan paused by Ms Darbus's desk, clearly enjoying the feeling that all eyes were on them. They even seemed to be striking a pose, as if they had just made their entrance onto a Broadway stage.

"You're late," Ms Darbus said, frowning. Even though Sharpay and Ryan were the stars of the Drama Club, and even though Ms Darbus was the drama teacher, she still didn't like lateness. "And I must say, I'm very surprised at you both! Surely your years of theatre training under my direction, no less, would have taught you that punctuality is a key component to success!"

"Yes, you're right and we're *soooo* sorry!" Sharpay exclaimed, her eyes widening in dismay. "But we have an incredibly good reason!"

Ryan nodded eagerly. "We just happened to be walking past Principal Matsui's office," he broke in. "And Mr Matsui just happened to see us. And then he just happened to say –"

"That I was the perfect person to introduce a new student to our homeroom!" Sharpay interrupted, shooting an irritated glance at her brother.

Ryan bit his lip and took a couple of steps backward. He knew better than to try to steal Sharpay's spotlight, but sometimes he just couldn't help himself. Like now, when they had such an exciting announcement to make!

"And that new student is —" Sharpay flung open the classroom door with all the dramatic flair she could muster. "— Jean-Luc Laurent, from Paris, France!"

Everyone in the class leaned forward in their seats as Jean-Luc walked in with an easy stride.

"Ta-da!" Sharpay cried, holding both arms out toward him as if she were a game-show host and he were the grand prize.

He looked a little taken aback by her greeting, but he smiled easily at the class.

"Bonjour," he said. "I mean, hello."

Gabriella couldn't help exchanging a quick glance with Taylor, who gave her a look that said that she, too, was impressed. Jean-Luc had dark brown hair, brown eyes, and a confident smile.

He didn't seem at all nervous as he stood in front of a room full of strangers. He was wearing jeans and a white shirt, which should have looked just, well, ordinary. But instead, Gabriella thought he looked casual, glamourous, and somehow very... French.

She looked around and noticed that every girl in the class was staring at Jean-Luc intently.

"*Bonjour!* We are, er, *très content* to have you here!" Ms Darbus cried as she rushed forward to shake his hand.

DESTINED FOR STARDOM!

Sharpay never turns down a chance to SHINE. Sharpay. She's been the star of pretty much every play and musical East High has staged since she was a freshman. Whether she's PERFORMING on stage, singing in her pop group, campaigning to become Spirit Queen or planning parties, Sharpay usually gets what she wants. A lot of being a *star* is about giving off the right vibe – if you believe you're awesome, everyone else will too!

Queen of Lava Springs

celeb spotting!

Sharpay is just waiting for the day that she's a bona fide star, so she's always on the lookout for fellow *celebs* to hang out with. A good place to star spot is at her parent's Lava Springs Country Club where celebrities sometimes drop in for a spot of pampering and relaxation. When Sharpay gets the opportunity, she visits the SWANKIEST restaurants and best DESIGNER stores – anywhere that celebrities might go.

Shopping!

One of Sharpay's favourite things in the world is shopping! She just can't get enough and wholeheartedly subscribes to the theory you can never have too many CLOTHES or accessories. Sharpay's a real STYLE chameleon and she's always looking through magazines for celebrity images to copy. But although Sharpay follows fashion and the latest TRENDS, she only wears clothes that suit her and make her feel confident.

RELAXING!

One of Sharpay's favourite ways to CHILL OUT is by getting a facial at the Lava Springs Country Club. It's because Sharpay understands it's important to look after her skin and keep her complexion GLOWING. To help keep her skin in tip-top condition, Sharpay eats healthily, drinks tons of water and makes sure she gets plenty of beauty sleep.